PICTURE
BOOK

2022

D0493703

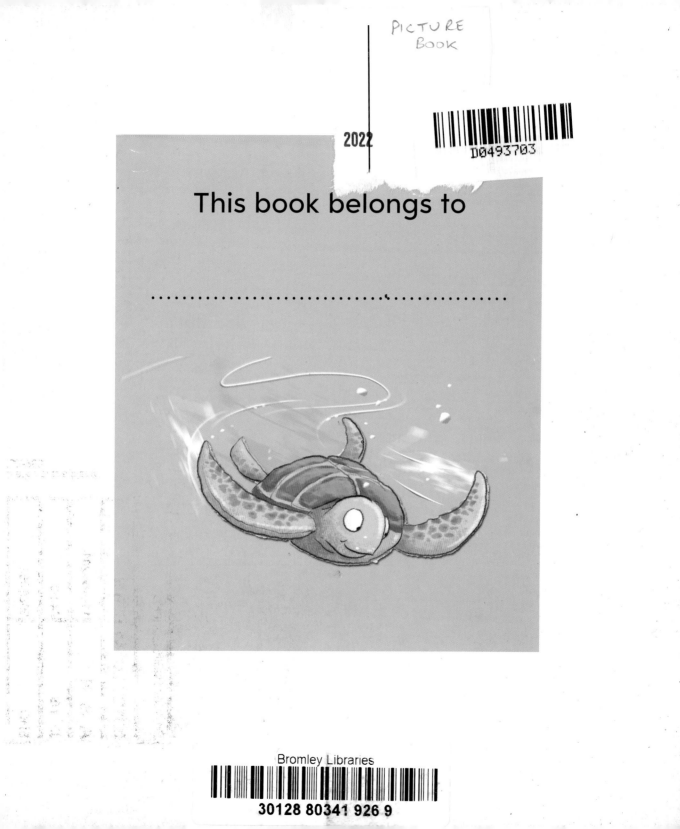

This book belongs to

....

Bromley Libraries

30128 80341 926 9

Quarto Knows

Quarto is the authority on a wide range of topics.

Quarto educates, entertains and enriches the lives of our readers—enthusiasts and lovers of hands-on living.

www.quartoknows.com

© 2018 Quarto Publishing plc

First published in 2018 by QED Publishing,
an imprint of The Quarto Group.
The Old Brewery, 6 Blundell Street,
London N7 9BH, United Kingdom.
T (0)20 7700 6700 F (0)20 7700 8066
www.QuartoKnows.com

All rights reserved. No part of this publication may be reproduced, stored in a retrieval system, or transmitted in any form or by any means, electronic, mechanical, photocopying, recording, or otherwise, without the prior permission of the publisher, nor be otherwise circulated in any form of binding or cover other than that in which it is published and without a similar condition being imposed on the subsequent purchaser.

A catalogue record for this book is available from the British Library.

ISBN 978-1-78493-928-1

Based on the original story by A. H. Benjamin and Bill Bolton
Author of adapted text: Katie Woolley
Series Editor: Joyce Bentley
Series Designer: Sarah Peden

Manufactured in Dongguan, China TL102017

9 8 7 6 5 4 3 2 1

FSC
www.fsc.org

MIX
Paper from responsible sources
FSC® C104723

Shark lives in a sunken ship at the bottom of the sea.

He is lonely all by himself.

"I just want some friends," says Shark.

One day, Shark has an idea. He heads out to find some friends.

Octopus swims by. He has long arms that go splish, splash, splosh!

"Got you!" shouts Shark. He puts Octopus in a bag.

Shark hides in the seaweed.

Lobster comes along. His claws go click, clack, clickety-clack!

"Got you!" snaps Shark. He puts Lobster in the bag, too.

"Oh no!" cries Lobster.

Shark hides inside
a dark cave.

It's not long until
Turtle swims past.
His flippers go flip,
flap, flop!

Shark leaps out of the cave!

"Got you!" he laughs. He puts Turtle in the bag.

Just then, Jellyfish wobbles past.
Swish, swash, swoosh!

Shark pounces out from behind
the sand!

"Got you too!" he says.

"Let me out!" shouts Jellyfish.

Shark's bag is getting very full!

Shark is having such fun. He wants to find more friends. He hides in a deep hole.

Starfish crawls past the hole. Shark jumps out and stuffs Starfish into the bag too.

"Time to go home," says Shark. "I'm hungry!"

Octopus, Lobster, Turtle, Jellyfish and Starfish are all in Shark's bag.

"Shark is going to eat us for lunch," cries Jellyfish.

Back inside the sunken ship,
Shark opens the bag.

"Hello, everyone!" he says. "Welcome
to my home!"

"Please don't eat us for lunch!" shouts Lobster. Shark goes into the kitchen...

"Surprise!" shouts Shark. "I made a cake for you all!"

"It looks delicious!" says Turtle.

"I like cake," says Lobster.

"Next time you want us round for cake, you can just ask!" says Octopus.

So Shark did!

Story Words

bag

cake

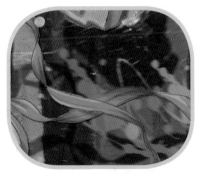

cave

hole

jellyfish

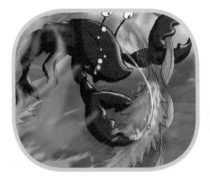

lobster

octopus

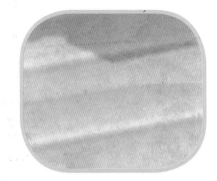

sand

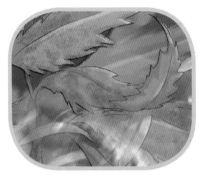

seaweed

shark

ship

starfish

turtle

25

Let's Talk About Shark Wants a Friend

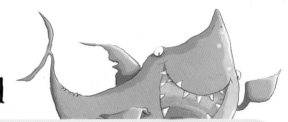

Look carefully at the book cover.

Who can you see in the picture?

What do you think each of the characters are feeling?

Lots of creatures live in the sea.

Can you remember which animals are in this story?

Do you have a favourite?

The animals are all trapped in Shark's bag.

Look at their faces.
How are they feeling?

How do you think Shark is feeling?

Do you think Shark goes about making friends in the right way?

What other ways could he have tried to make friends?

What happens at the end of the story?

Did you like the ending?

Fun and Games

Sound out the letters and read the words.
Find the objects in the big picture.

fish   sea   shell   coins   teeth

chair   seaweed   bubbles

Choose the correct word to complete these sentences.

hides   ship   bag   cake

Shark lives in a sunken .... at the bottom of the sea.

He puts octopus in a ....

Next, Shark .... in the seaweed.

"I made a .... for you all!"

Your Turn

Now that you have read the story,
have a go at telling it in your own words.
Use the pictures below to help you.

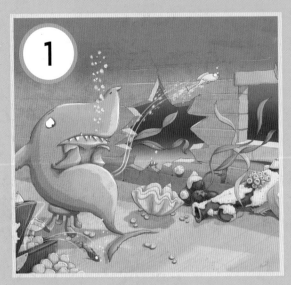

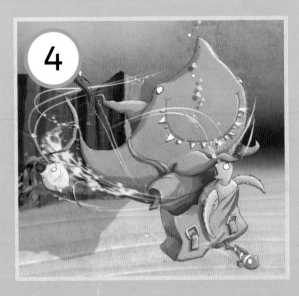

GET TO KNOW READING GEMS

Reading Gems is a series of books that has been written for children who are learning to read. The books have been created in consultation with a literacy and teaching specialist.

The books fit into four levels, with each level getting more challenging as a child's confidence and reading ability grows. The simple text and fun illustrations provide gradual, structured practice of reading. Most importantly, these books are good stories that are fun to read!

Level 1 is for children who are taking their first steps into reading. Story themes and subjects are familiar to young children, and there is lots of repetition to build reading confidence.

Level 2 is for children who have taken their first reading steps and are becoming readers. Story themes are still familiar but sentences are a bit longer, as children begin to tackle more challenging vocabulary.

Level 3 is for children who are developing as readers. Stories and subjects are varied, and more descriptive words are introduced.

Level 4 is for readers who are rapidly growing in reading confidence and independence. There is less repetition on the page, broader themes are explored and plot lines straddle multiple pages.

Shark Wants a Friend follows Shark as he goes in search of friends. It explores themes of sea creatures and friendship.

Level 3

"It looks delicious!" says Turtle.
"I like cake," says Lobster.

"Next time you want us round for cake, you can just ask!" says Octopus.
So Shark did!

Longer sentences ✓

Varied language ✓

Wider vocabulary ✓

Pictures and words support one another ✓